New Girl

by Janet Adele Bloss

To my parents —
With love and affection.

Cover photo by Bichsel Morris
Photographic Illustrators.

Published by Willowisp Press, Inc.
401 E. Wilson Bridge Road, Worthington, Ohio 43085

Printed in the United States of America
10 9 8 7 6

ISBN 0-87406-048-6

1

Molly Adams was miserable. She didn't have winter boots and the slick soles of her shoes slipped over the icy sidewalk. She fell, dropping her new notebooks into the snow.

"Ouch!" she yelled. She stood up and brushed the snow from her bruised knees.

"What an awful day! What a gross town! What weird weather with all this messy snow and slush! What could be worse?" she asked herself.

Molly could think of only one thing worse than all the snow, ice and bruised knees put together. That one thing was moving to a new town and going to a new school for the very first time . . . a new school where she didn't know one single person.

And that's exactly what Molly Adams was doing this wintry November morning. She was slipping and sliding along to her first day at Ballard Junior High School. This was a school where she didn't know anyone, not *one single* person.

Molly Adams was a new girl in town. She had only been in Ballard, Minnesota, for two days. Her dad already had been here for a month. He had come early to find a house for the Adams' family.

Mr. Adams had already started his job at the Smith-Glass Plant, Inc. The Arizona branch of Smith-Glass had promoted him to Executive Sales Director. Molly wasn't sure what exactly her dad would be doing in this position, but her parents were very happy about it.

Mr. Adams had come home one October evening back in Arizona with a big smile on his face. He threw open the front door and yelled, "All right! Everybody out! We're going to dinner at the best restaurant in town!"

"Jack, what is it?" Molly's mother cried as she ran into the room.

"I got it! I got it!" Mr. Adams said excitedly. "The phone call came today!"

"Oh, Jack! I'm so happy for you!" Mrs. Adams hugged him and they danced around the room.

Molly could still remember the whole scene. At first she didn't know what her parents were so excited about. But her older brother, Jeff, came racing into the room and clapped their dad on the back. "Congratulations on your new job," Jeff said.

New job? Molly wondered. Was that good or

bad? She wasn't sure.

"Dad," Molly asked. "Will we have to move?"

"I'm afraid so, punkin," Mr. Adams said. "We'll be moving to Minnesota. You'll like it there. There are lots of trees and beautiful hills."

"Yippee!" cried Jeff. "I'll learn how to snow ski!"

"I can ski, too. Me, too! Me, too!" little Wendy cried. The five-year-old ran to her father and hugged his knees. She looked over at her older sister, Molly, and said again, "I can ski, too!"

"You're too little for that right now, my girl," Mr. Adams said. "But you can build a snowman."

That was one month ago. Now, Molly was living in Ballard, Minnesota. It all seemed to happen so fast. Before Molly left Arizona, she said good-bye to all her friends, especially Vickie, on her last day at school in Carlene. They'd been best friends forever. They promised to write letters every week.

Being a cheerleader was one of the most exciting things in Molly's life. So she cried when she turned in her cheerleading pom-poms. It was right before basketball season, too. Molly loved the warm smell and feel of the gymnasium during basketball games. She loved to leap and twirl with the other cheerleaders. But that was all over now. Brenda Vosta, the alternate, was taking Molly's place on the squad.

That was four days ago. Molly sighed. Just four days ago she was in sunny Arizona and now . . . now . . . Oops! She slipped again, falling into a snow drift.

Ballard Junior High School wasn't far from her new home. But walking in the ice and snow made it seem like a long way.

Molly thought about her brother, Jeff. He was a sophomore and two years older. He'd left on the bus that morning for the high school. The high school was farther away than the junior high school. So Jeff didn't have to walk the distance like Molly did.

Moving didn't seem to bother Jeff. All he could talk about was skiing and basketball. And little Wendy was perfectly happy to make piles of snowballs all over the yard. She even cried when her mother made her come back into the house to warm up and get dry mittens.

What's the big deal about snow? Molly wondered. It's wet, it's cold and it gets in my shoes. Her teeth chattered as she crossed the icy street. "How does anyone walk on this stuff?" she mumbled to herself. Clouds of vapor puffed from her mouth with each word.

Molly wasn't used to snow. In fact, the snow in Ballard was the very first snow Molly had ever seen; the first *real* snow anyway. Molly had seen snow in Carlene twice in her 13 years. But those snows were just little fluffy flakes that fell here and there, melting as soon as they hit the ground. When it snowed in Carlene all the kids in school ran out to see it because snow was so unusual for that southwestern part of the state. For the most part Carlene stayed dry and warm. The desert stretched around the town, reflecting the sun and warming the cacti and desert flowers in the summer. It got cool in the winter evenings, but nothing like this! Molly shivered.

She stopped walking and looked up. There it was, Ballard Junior High School. It looked so big. Sunlight and snow reflected in the rows of windows. Other kids hurried up the steps to the front door, clutching their books under their arms. Most of them walked in pairs or groups. Molly was the only one who climbed the cement stairs alone. Her feet crunched with each step as she walked on salt crystals scattered around to melt the snow. Molly noticed that she was the only one not wearing boots. And she was the only one wearing a light jacket. All the other kids wore heavy coats and woolen scarves wrapped around their chins. She couldn't see their faces. Only eyes peeped through the space between neck scarves and knitted hats.

Molly entered the front door. Students rushed every which way. Lockers slammed and voices shouted over the din.

Molly checked the registration paper she had safely tucked away in her purse. It listed the room numbers of classes that she was to take. First on the list was homeroom in room 212 with Mrs. Fister.

Molly joined the hurrying students in the hall. She climbed the stairs wedged between a girl in jeans and a short boy with curly brown hair. Molly stopped by room 212 and peered through the door. She hoped nobody could hear her heart pounding.

Then Molly walked into the room. Conversations stopped and curious eyes from around the classroom stared at her.

"You must be our new student," Mrs. Fister said. "Molly Adams?"

Molly nodded her head and said, "Yes, ma'am." She noticed that Mrs. Fister had gray hair streaked with white. Her voice was kind.

"Class! Class!" Mrs. Fister called. "I'd like for you to meet our new student, Molly Adams. Where are you from, dear?" Mrs. Fister asked.

"Arizona," Molly said. "Carlene, Arizona." Her voice was quiet and Molly hoped that she didn't sound too nervous.

"Arizona?" Mrs. Fister said. "My! That's a long way from here. It's almost another world! Well, Molly, I hope you'll like Minnesota. Class! Please make Molly feel welcome and help her find her way around." Mrs. Fister smiled. "Just take a seat, Molly, and then I'll call roll."

Molly looked around for an empty desk. There was one in the back of the room. She held her notebooks close against her as she walked down the aisle. The floor was wet with slush and snow that dripped from students' boots.

Suddenly, the slick soles of Molly's shoes shot out from under her. Molly tried to regain her balance, but couldn't. Her notebooks flew into the air as she threw her arms up. Her knee twisted as she fell. She abruptly sat in the floor's gray slush.

Nearby students jumped up to help her. Mrs. Fister rushed to her side while titters of laughter erupted around the room. Molly heard someone ask, "Is that how they walk in Arizona?" She heard another voice say, "What a klutz!"

Molly pushed herself up off the floor and gathered her notebooks. The seat of her skirt was wet and cold. It clung to the back of her legs and felt awful. She looked down at her socks which were now streaked with gray.

"It's that wet floor. We'll get the janitor to mop it up. Are you all right? Oh, dear. You'll need to wash up," Mrs. Fister chattered. "The restroom is just down the hall."

Molly left the room feeling like a giraffe at a chipmunk party. She knew she stuck out like a sore thumb. She could hear laughter coming from the classroom as she walked down the hall. Her skirt, still sticking to her legs, made a *thwap* sound with each step she took. Molly was afraid that someone was going to see her and think she wet her pants like some little kids do in grade school. But the hall was empty.

In the bathroom, Molly washed her legs and wrung out the back of her skirt. She looked into the mirror at her bright, brown eyes.

"Now you've done it," she mumbled to herself. "Everyone's laughing at you and at your stupid shoes. You've made a complete clown of yourself. Oh, I wish Vickie was here. I wish I was back in Carlene."

The hardest part was returning to the classroom. No one laughed. No one even smiled. Had Mrs. Fister said something to them? Molly wondered.

Molly sat at her desk and thought about the rest of the day. It *had* to get better. It *can't* get any worse, can it? Molly frowned.

Molly found her way to the cafeteria at lunchtime. The cooks were serving hot dogs and sauerkraut, so Molly just took a carton of milk and a peach cobbler. Molly wouldn't eat sauerkraut for anything. She didn't like the smell of it.

She took her tray and sat at the end of a long table. The kids at the other end looked at her, then back at each other and continued talking.

It was embarrassing to eat alone. She felt like such a wallflower. Molly tried to smile so that she wouldn't look so nervous. But it was hard to smile and eat peach cobbler at the same time. And anyway, Molly thought, it might look dumb. This peach cobbler, all sweet and soupy, was nothing to smile about.

Molly heard a girl's voice behind her say, "There's nowhere else to sit. Let's sit here. Marge's table is full. Come on. This is the only place left."

A chair was pulled out beside her. Molly turned to see a pretty blonde-haired girl in a cheerleading uniform sit beside her. Her pleated skirt showed the blue and yellow colors of the school.

"Hi," said Molly shyly.

"Oh, hi," said the girl.

The cheerleader's friend sat in the empty chair across from Molly.

"Hi," Molly said to her. She wanted to kick herself under the table for not being able to think of anything else to say.

"Are you new?" the girl asked.

"Yes, I'm Molly Adams. This is my first day."

"Welcome to the pit of the universe," said the cheerleader. "My name's Arlene. Arlene Schwartz. Why in the world did you ever move to this dumpy town?"

"My dad got a job here," Molly said. "So did my mom."

Arlene turned to her food and began to eat.

"I was a cheerleader, too," Molly said, "back in Carlene, Arizona." She grinned, hoping this fact would start a conversation with Arlene.

"Really?" said Arlene. She yawned. Then she hunched her shoulders and leaned across the table, talking to her friend. They whispered back and forth.

Molly returned to her peach cobbler which she ate as slowly as possible. She had to make it last a long time. She didn't want to be left sitting there with no one to talk to and nothing to do.

Why is Arlene so unfriendly? Or is it just my imagination? Molly wondered. She hoped the story about her falling down in homeroom hadn't spread over the whole school.

Molly finished her dessert as the bell rang. Arlene and her friend got up from the table.

"Bye," said Molly. "It was nice to meet you."

Maybe the two girls didn't hear her. They didn't say anything. They didn't even look at Molly. Instead, they just walked into the crowd of hurrying students and disappeared.

Molly looked at all the strange faces around her. I don't think I'm going to like this place, she thought to herself.

2

"And the cutest girl sits in front of me in history," Jeff said. "She has the reddest hair and the greenest eyes I've ever seen. Pass the gravy, please." He spooned more gravy onto his potatoes. "Yup," he said with a satisfied grin. "Not bad for a first day. Not bad at all."

It was dinner time in the Adams' home. Molly wished she could stuff cotton in her ears or in her brother's mouth. So far all he could talk about was how great Ballard High School was and how great the guys in gym class were. He liked the redheaded girl. He liked his teachers. He talked with the basketball coach and he was going to try out for the team, the "Ballard Braves."

With his mouth full of potatoes, Jeff excitedly began talking again about the basketball coach. "I told him I played center in Carlene," Jeff explained. "Coach Lemler said they need a center. But first I have to prove myself. I'm practicing with the guys after school tomorrow."

"Well, you're certainly tall enough," Mrs. Adams said. "I hope you make it."

"How did *your* first day go, hon?" Mr. Adams asked looking at his wife. "Was work all right?"

"I need to read some systems manuals," Mrs. Adams said. "But I think I'll be okay. The job is similar to what I was doing in Carlene, only I need to learn about the particular system this company uses."

Mrs. Adams was a computer programmer. She'd had very little trouble finding a job in Ballard. She flew up to interview with the town's bus company, the Ballard Transit Company (BTC). She was hired on the spot and flew back to Carlene with the news. That was just two weeks before she, Molly, Jeff, and Wendy left Carlene to join Mr. Adams in Ballard.

"What are you doing at BTC, Mom?" Jeff asked. "Making the buses go to the moon?"

Mrs. Adams laughed. "I'm writing a program that will route the buses and calculate the time it takes them to get from one place to another. It'll figure out how much they spend on gasoline, too."

"Whew!" said Jeff. "It sounds pretty complicated."

"What about you, Wendy-love?" asked Mr. Adams. "How was your first day in your new

14

kindergarten? Did you have fun?"

"We got chocolate cookies with faces on them," Wendy said. "Mine had an elephant face and I ate three." The little girl wriggled her bottom on the phone book and cushion that allowed her to reach the table. "I colored with Sara Jane," she said.

"Who's Sara Jane?" asked Mrs. Adams.

"My best friend. We both wore blue socks," Wendy giggled.

"Well, that's a pretty good reason to be friends," Mr. Adams said. "Some of my best friends wear blue socks." He laughed. So did Mrs. Adams and Jeff.

Molly buttered a roll and took a tiny bite of it. How can they act like this? she thought. They all act like they like it here. They act like they don't even miss Carlene.

Molly felt very alone as she sat at the dinner table with her family around her. She hoped that they wouldn't ask her about her day. How could she tell them that she slipped and sat in a puddle? How could she tell them that the whole class laughed at her and someone called her a klutz and no one would talk to her at lunchtime?

It was all so strange here. Back in Carlene she was a cheerleader and had lots of friends. She grew up with Vickie and they knew everything about each other. They never kept secrets.

15

Nobody in the whole world knew Molly like Vickie did, not even Molly's parents.

"So, Molly, as long as we're taking a family survey, how was *your* day?" Mr. Adams asked.

"Okay," she said.

"Just okay?" Her parents and Jeff looked at her.

Molly didn't know what else to say. She stared at the pork chop on her plate.

"Did you meet anyone new?" Jeff asked. "Any cute guys in your classes? Did you show them your cheerleading stuff?"

"Cut it out, Jeff!" yelled Molly. She was surprised at her own voice and how angry she sounded.

"Leave your sister alone, Jeff," Mrs. Adams said. "You know better than to tease her."

"Did you have a rough day, honey?" Molly's mother asked gently. She reached out and put her hand over Molly's hand.

Molly's eyes filled with tears. She'd had the worst day of her life. But she didn't want to tell anyone, at least not anyone in her family. There was only one person she could tell. And that person was thousands of miles away.

"May I be excused?" Molly asked.

"Of course," Mrs. Adams said. "Why don't you just take it easy this evening? Tomorrow will be better."

Molly pushed her chair back from the table. How can she say that? Molly wondered. How can she know that tomorrow will be better than today? Maybe tomorrow will be *worse* than today. But today certainly felt like the worst, ever, she thought to herself.

Molly walked to her bedroom. She closed the door and sat at her writing table. She took a piece of stationery and began to write:

Dear Vickie,

Ballard is the worst town in the world. It really stinks. Today was my first day at school. Everything went wrong. Everyone here is a creep. This town is so dumb that they have to wear special boots to walk in the snow. And there's snow everywhere!!! It even melts on the floors in the school classrooms. You almost have to swim to your desk.

I miss you and living in Carlene a lot. Has Brenda Vosta taken my place on the squad yet? I met a cheerleader today named Arlene. She was a snob and not half as nice as we always were.

Mom says I can visit Carlene this summer. I can't wait to see you.

Your sad friend,
Molly

P.S. Tell Brenda that I've seen her do the Victory Yell and she needs to jump a little higher.

Molly folded the letter and put it in an envelope. She looked around her bedroom and felt like it wasn't really hers. She missed her bulletin board that had cheerleading pictures and photos of her Carlene friends pinned to it. It held ticket stubs from putt-putt games and movies that she and Vickie had gone to.

"No," Molly said to herself. "This isn't really my room."

She felt it couldn't be her room, yet. No secrets

had been shared here, no late night giggling under the blankets with her girl friends who slept over. Her bulletin board wasn't on the wall, yet. An unfamiliar landscape stretched outside her window.

Molly's eyes fell on her math book and she remembered that she had homework to do. Math class had been terrible today. The teacher, Mr. Beggid, was bald and skinny. He spent the entire period talking about percentages and formulas. Molly didn't understand what in the world he was talking about. She didn't ask questions because she didn't want the kids in the class to think she was stupid. That kind of math chatter sounded similar to the times when her mom talked with other programmers about computer stuff. It reminded Molly of Chinese, but with lots of numbers.

Yuk! Math wasn't half this hard in Carlene. Molly opened her book to the first homework problem. It read:

A loaded truck weighs 20,000 lbs. If 80% of this represents the load, how much does the truck weigh?

Molly stared at the problem. How in the world did Mr. Beggid think of this problem? she wondered.

Numbers and words whirled in Molly's head. She looked ahead at the other problems. There were 14 more to do and they looked harder. Molly closed the book. She remembered back to dinner time when her mother said, "Why don't you just take it easy this evening?"

"Well, maybe I should listen to my mom," she said to herself. Molly put her math book away.

She took more paper from her desk and began to write again.

Dear Vickie,

I know I just wrote to you, but I have some time before I go to bed. So, I thought I'd write some more.

The math class here is very hard. I think we're doing high school stuff instead of eighth grade stuff. You have to be a genius to do it.

Did I tell you that I hate this town? Ballard is the pits!

Your lonely friend,
Molly

3

Mr. Beggid stood in front of the class with a piece of chalk in his hand. Sunlight from the window made his bald head shine a pinkish color.

"Molly Adams," he called. "Miss Adams, would you please come up to the front and show us how you worked problem 12 from last night's homework?"

Molly felt her stomach do a flip-flop. She knew she couldn't do problem 12 because she hadn't even done problem 1.

It's at times like these, Molly thought, that I wish I lived on Mars. Molly figured that if anyone really lived on Mars they would probably never go to school and they definitely would not have to do math homework.

"Is something wrong, Miss Adams?" Mr. Beggid asked. He opened his eyes very wide when he said the word "wrong."

Molly felt her face growing hot. She thought everyone was probably staring at her. She looked down at the desk. She heard Mr. Beggid's voice coming from the front of the room.

"Did you perhaps not complete your homework assignment for last night?" he asked.

"No, sir," Molly said quietly.

"Is that 'no, sir' you did complete it or 'no, sir' you did not complete it?"

Molly was confused. "No, sir," she said. "I didn't do it."

"Well, perhaps you'll show me what you *have* done," he said. "Please bring your homework to me."

Molly wanted to cry. But she couldn't, not here, not in front of everyone. "I don't have any homework," she confessed. "I didn't do it."

Mr. Beggid looked around the class. "Is there anyone else here who did not at least *try* to do last night's homework?" he asked. "Please raise your hand if you didn't."

All the students turned their heads to see who would raise their hand, but no one did.

"It appears, Miss Adams, that you are the only one in the entire class who did not even try. If you need help, let me know. I'm sure we could arrange something for you." He stared for a moment at Molly where she sat, then continued speaking. "I will not tolerate laziness in my class.

Tina Burris, please come to the board and do problem 12."

A thin girl with short brown hair walked to the front. She held her homework in her hand.

As Tina wrote numbers on the board, Molly sat in embarrassed silence. She thought about how the other kids probably thought she was super dumb, thanks to Mr. Beggid. She thought that teachers in Carlene were never this mean. Never!

"Class, don't forget the math test this Thursday," Mr. Beggid said. "It will cover the second chapter. I hope the entire class will be prepared for it."

He seemed to be staring right at Molly.

The bell rang. All the other students hopped up and rushed out. Molly moved slowly because she didn't want anyone to look at her. She was tired of people staring at her just because she was new. But someone *was* looking at her when she walked through the door into the hall.

It was Tina Burris. Tina stood with her books in her arms, leaning against the wall. "Hi," she said. "Do you have lunch now?"

"Yeah," said Molly, looking up in surprise.

"Want to eat with me?" Tina asked.

"Sure." Molly walked beside Tina. She couldn't thing of anything to say because she was still shaken up by math class and Mr. Beggid.

"Hey," said Tina, smiling. "Don't let Mr. Egghead get to you. He can be a real bear. Maybe he had a crummy breakfast this morning and that's why he was so grouchy." She smiled. "Maybe he burned his toast."

Molly laughed. "If anything got burned it was *me* just now in that class," she said.

Tina giggled. "I know what you mean," she said. "That must have been awful."

They walked into the cafeteria and stood in line with their trays. After they got their food, they sat at a long table by the window. The seats around them filled up quickly.

"This stuff is gross," Tina said, gazing at the lunch before her. "The cooks call it Shepherd's Pie, but we call it 'Layered Leftovers.' "

Molly took a fork and tasted it. "We had something like this in Carlene," she commented. "Only we called it 'Mystery Mess.' "

"That's a good one," Tina said. "Say, where's Carlene? Is it south? You have kind of an accent."

"It's in Arizona," Molly said. "It's really a neat town. There's desert nearby Carlene and we used to hike around there. We had to be real careful to take water with us if we were out there for very long. It gets real hot in the summer.

"The cacti are beautiful when they flower in spring. There's one called 'Horse crippler.' It's a terrible name, but it's real pretty with long spikes and pink flowers."

"A hot desert sounds real good right now," Tina said. "Br-r-r-r-r! What do you think of all this snow?"

Molly didn't want to say she hated it because that wouldn't be nice. But she didn't want to say she liked it because that would be a lie. "I'm still getting used to it," she said. "It's different."

"Do you ski?" Tina asked.

"Snow ski? No," said Molly. "This is the first time I've been around snow."

"Really? I'll teach you to ski if you like," Tina said.

"Sure," said Molly. But she didn't really want to learn. She figured if she had such a hard time walking on the stuff in regular shoes, there's no way she could slide down a hill with two boards strapped to her feet.

"There are some great places to ski around here," Tina said. "Maybe we could do some backpacking."

Molly sipped her chocolate milk, then said, "I like to backpack. In Carlene we used to take a picnic lunch and walk along the Pecos Creek looking for Indian arrowheads. There used to be Indians all over the place out there," she explained.

Just then Arlene, the cheerleader, walked by

the table with her tray. She looked down at Tina and said, "Hi, Tina. How's it going?"

"Okay," Tina said. "How's practice coming? You ready for the big game?"

"Yeah, I guess so," said Arlene. "We still need to practice the pyramid, though."

"I could help you with that," Molly offered. "We used to do the pyramid in Carlene."

"No thanks," Arlene said. She turned and left.

Molly watched her walk away. It seemed to her that Arlene didn't like her very much. But she couldn't figure out why. She doesn't even know me, Molly thought.

Tina was eating her dessert, chocolate pudding.

"I was a cheerleader in Carlene," Molly explained. "We had eight people on the squad. I moved right before basketball season started so I missed the first big Pep Rally. The school had it on the same day that my family moved here."

"This pudding is gross," Tina said, wrinkling her nose. "I wonder if one of the cooks dropped his underwear in it or something. Yuk!"

"Our basketball team won the state championship in Carlene for two years in a row," Molly said. "Carlene has a good football team, too."

The bell rang for class to begin again.

"I'd better hurry," said Tina. "I've got history now." She jumped up and rushed off into the crowd.

Molly stood and looked at the sea of strange faces around her. "Alone again," she said to herself. "I wonder if Tina likes me. Arlene doesn't like me. Maybe I talk about Carlene too much. I guess I should learn to keep my big mouth shut about Carlene."

Molly carried her tray to the dirty dish window. She turned to the door where students were rushing out. Over the noise she heard a voice call, "Molly! Molly!" It was Tina's voice, but Molly couldn't see her face in the crowd.

"What?" Molly called back.

"I'll meet you at your locker after school, okay? Want to come over to my house for some hot cocoa?" Tina yelled.

"Sure!" Molly shouted into the crowd. "I'd love to! See you then!"

Molly walked to English class with a smile on her face. Suddenly, the afternoon looked brighter. And it was all because of Tina, Molly's first friend in Ballard.

4

Molly woke up with a sick feeling in her stomach. She knew it wasn't something she ate. And she knew she wasn't really sick. The bad feeling came from knowing that Mr. Egghead was handing back the tests they'd taken. Molly wasn't sure how she'd done. There was one question about fractions that she didn't even try. It was impossible.

Molly ate her breakfast in silence, then clomped through the snow on her way to school. At least she had some new snow boots to wear. They made it easier for her to keep from falling down. But her feet felt like they weighed 50 pounds apiece. They were so clunky!

During math class Molly couldn't listen to what Mr. Egghead was saying. She was too busy worrying about her test score. She hoped that no one would see her score when the tests were given back. Paul Derryvane, who sat next to her, was a straight-A student. He might laugh when he saw all the red marks on her paper. Even though he looked like a nerd, Molly still didn't want him to laugh at her.

Maybe it's not so bad, Molly thought hopefully. I've been doing some of my homework, so maybe I did okay. I just might surprise myself.

Mr. Beggid stood before the class with a stack of papers in his hand.

"Class," he said. "Here are your tests from last week. I was very pleased with most of the scores."

As the papers were passed over, Molly kept an eye on Paul to see if he peeked at her score.

He did. That nerd! But he didn't laugh. Maybe that was a good sign. He passed the stack to Molly. She squinted her eyes before she looked at her score. She opened her eyes bit by bit.

At the top of the paper she saw a big red "F." *F*!!! Molly hurriedly flipped the paper over, *F*-side down. She couldn't believe it. She'd never failed a test before, never ever! *F*! What would her parents say?

Molly's heart began to beat faster and her stomach felt like it was doing somersaults. She wondered if she was going to throw up. Maybe she should, all over her test. But no, she reasoned. Barfing was no way to win friends.

"Class!" said Mr. Beggid. "As I said before,

the grades were for the most part quite good. We only had one *F* and three *D's*."

Molly hoped that no one would look at her and know she was the one who had made the only *F*. *The only F*! She wondered if that meant she was the dumbest one in the class.

Paul Derryvane knew she'd made an *F*. He was the only other student who knew. Molly wondered if he could keep his mouth shut about it. But it was hard to tell with someone who looked the way Paul did.

He looked so pale. But then *everyone* looked a little pale in Minnesota. It seemed like people in Carlene didn't look as pasty as the kids in Ballard.

The rest of the day dragged for Molly. She hid the test in the gym bag she kept in her locker.

Ann Jelway, a girl in Molly's math class, asked her how she did on the test. So did Steve Brady. Molly pretended she didn't hear them. It was the first time either of them had spoken to her. Molly wished they'd said something else like, "Hey! I love your skirt!" or "Let's get together this weekend. There's a great flick downtown."

Molly kicked at the snow on her way home after school. Each time she kicked, she pretended it was Mr. Egghead. But she banged her toe when a snow drift she kicked turned out to be covering a fire hydrant.

"Ow!" she yelled and hopped on one foot. Tears welled up in her eyes.

Her parents weren't home from work yet when Molly got home. Jeff had picked Wendy up at the sitter's and the two of them were in the kitchen munching on potato chips.

"Hey, squirt!" Jeff said when Molly came in the door. "How was school? Have they kicked you out, yet?" Jeff and Wendy laughed.

"Go jump in a lake," Molly said.

"There's a letter for you on the table," said Jeff. "It's from Ickie."

Molly ran to get it. She knew that Jeff meant Vickie. He said that to make her mad. Back in Carlene he always called the two of them Moldy and Ickie.

The envelope was yellow with golden daisies on it. It made Molly think of sunshine, desert and bright, blooming cactus flowers (all the things that Carlene had that Ballard didn't!). She took the letter to her bedroom and closed the door. A letter from home, her *real* home, was something to be read in private.

Before Molly opened it, she took the math test from her gym bag. She smoothed the wrinkles out of it, folded it up, then stuck it under her mattress. There didn't seem to be much point in showing it to her parents. It would only upset them. Anyway, she'd do better on the next test.

Then Molly tore open the envelope and began to read Vickie's letter.

Dear Molly,

Can you believe it? We won another basketball game. The team's doing great! We had the best victory dance in the gym. We started the dance by doing a cheer for everyone there. All the players were there, too. Brenda did a back flip and everyone cheered and clapped. You would have loved it! Some people are even saying we're good enough to go to the Cheer-leading Championship in Phoenix.

How's everything in Ballard? How many new friends have you made? I hope you haven't forgotten us already.

The weather here was gross last week. For a while we thought it might snow.

Everyone was wearing jackets and gloves and it was real funny. It kind of made everyone look fat.

I found two more arrowheads the other day.

Brenda and Katie said to say "hi."

I can't wait to see you next summer! Bye.

Love,
Vickie

Molly put the letter back in the envelope. Somehow it just didn't make her feel better. Letters usually cheered her up, but not today. Maybe it was because of the *F* hidden under her bed. Or maybe it was because she didn't know how to do a back flip.

Molly went to her window and gazed out at the landscape. Drifts of white snow covered everything. There were white bumps in the front yard. Maybe they're covered bushes, Molly wondered. She realized for the first time that she'd never even seen her yard. She didn't know what was under all that snow.

White, white, white. White was everywhere and the sky was gray. Where was the color? Molly closed her eyes and remembered the blue sky of Arizona, blue as a robin's egg. She remembered misty-colored sage, brown tumbleweeds, rough green grass and the cacti in bloom. She imagined cacti with scarlet flowers or delicate pink blooms or bright yellow blossoms. And there were the rust-colored prairie dogs who stuck their cute little heads out of their tunnels, then popped them back in again.

A sound outside made Molly open her eyes. It was the crunch of her parents car driving over snow. They pulled into the driveway just as Jeff ran out the front door. Jeff had his gym bag slung over his shoulder. "Bye!" he yelled. "I'm off to practice."

Jeff had passed tryouts. He was now on the basketball team at Ballard High School. He played center which was supposed to be a great position. But he still hadn't played in a game, yet.

"A basketball star . . . big deal," Molly muttered.

Molly tried to be happy for Jeff. She knew how much it meant for him to be on the team. But she couldn't help feeling a little left out. Here he was having such a great time. And here *she* was sitting alone by her bedroom window, feeling sorry for herself and looking out at the endless snow.

Molly watched Jeff with envy. He ran down the sidewalk and disappeared into the gray haze. Gray and white. Everything was gray and white.

Molly leaned her forehead against the window pane. Her breath made a spot of moisture on the glass. She opened her mouth and breathed quickly making a larger spot. Then she took her finger and carefully wrote on it, BALLARD SPITINKS!!!

SPITINKS was what you got when you put PIT and STINKS together. And, she thought, if ever a town spitunk, that town was Ballard, Minnesota.

5

Molly and Tina sat on the couch sipping cocoa. They were looking through magazines at pictures of beautiful women in furs and evening gowns.

"Look at this one," Molly said. "Wow! Do you think *we'll* ever look like that?"

"I don't know," Tina said doubtfully. "Seems to me we have an awful lot of growing to do, if you know what I mean."

Molly knew.

"Her lips are too purple, anyway," Molly said, squinting her eyes critically at the photo. "Look at this one." She pointed to the magazine in her lap. "Wouldn't you like to have hair like that?" she giggled.

"What if the wind blew?" Tina laughed. "It would all cave in."

The girls talked and flipped the pages while little Wendy played on the floor with her doll.

She had the doll sitting in a truck. She was trying to make the truck crash into a pillow without the doll falling out.

Jeff was at basketball practice as usual. He was meeting some friends afterward at the Chili Parlor. Jill was going to be there, too. Jill was the girl with red hair and green eyes that Jeff sat behind in history class. He talked about her during dinner every night. It was enough to make you sick, Molly thought.

Molly had seen Jeff put a little bottle of after-shave lotion in his gym bag just before he left. She thought that was pretty weird because Jeff didn't shave very often. And from what Molly could see he probably wouldn't have to shave very often for a long time.

Molly wondered why it seemed so hard for her to make friends. Jeff already had about a million friends from school. He knew all the guys on the basketball team and he talked to people in his classes. It just didn't seem to bother him to be around new people.

Why? Oh, why? Molly wondered, do I have to be so shy. Why can't I be more like Jeff? He can talk to *anybody*. He even talked with the mailman on Saturday mornings. The mailman was fat and missing a front tooth. Molly thought that he looked goofy and she could never think of anything to say to him. But Jeff could. Jeff could have people talking and laughing in five seconds flat!

Molly sighed as she flipped a page in the magazine. She bet the ladies in these pictures weren't shy. They probably could talk to anyone they wanted to. And they probably had a million dates with a million of the most handsome guys in the world.

Tina was spending the afternoon with Molly while Molly's parents were out Christmas shopping. Christmas was less than two weeks away and schools were closed for the holidays. Mrs. Adams was excited and put Christmas decorations everywhere. There was even a silver glitter reindeer head in the bathroom.

When everyone laughed at her for being so excited, Mrs. Adams said, "I can't help it. This is the first white Christmas we've ever had."

Molly wondered what was so special about a white Christmas when every other day was white, too. She didn't understand what was so great about having "Jack Frost nipping at your nose." Molly was tired of having her nose nipped.

"I'm glad you're coming with us tomorrow," Tina said. "I think you'll really like skiing. My dad's a great teacher. He started teaching me when I was six years old."

Molly's face brightened. She was leaving with the Burris family for a week of skiing in the hills.

At last she was going to learn how to get around in this stupid snow. As Tina explained to her, her family went for a week every year during the Christmas holidays and she got to take one friend with her. Molly was excited and scared about the prospect of skiing for the first time. She hoped she wouldn't hurt herself. But she could hardly wait to go!

At last she'd have something exciting and fun to write about to Vickie. None of Molly's friends in Carlene had ever been snow skiing. They'd think it was neat!

"I got some new socks," Molly said. "And some long underwear like you told me. Are you sure I won't kill myself? Will there be any guys there?"

"Scads of them," Tina smiled. "There are guys all over the place. You'll love it. The cabin where we stay is real neat. There's a fireplace and we can roast marshmallows and hot dogs. We always have a good time. My dad brings his guitar and sings to us at night. It's great."

The sound of laughter came from outside. Molly, Tina, and Wendy ran to the window. A group of children were walking by, dragging their sleds behind them.

"That looks like fun," said Molly.

"Oh, it is. We can do some sledding up in the hills if you want. There's always a bunch of kids up there with their toboggans," said Tina. "We'll have a whole week of just playing in the snow and doing whatever we want to do. I think I like Christmas holidays the best! I'm always sad when it's over."

"*You're* sad!" Molly cried. "We're having a math exam as soon as we get back to school. I don't know what's going on in that class! Can you believe a math exam right after Christmas?"

"Yeah. That stinks, doesn't it?" Tina said. "Mr. Egghead still seems to be giving you a hard time."

"Yeah. He gets mad when I don't finish my homework. He says I should work extra hard for this exam coming up," Molly frowned. "I wish he'd quit picking on me."

"He's pretty strict. That's for sure," Tina groaned.

"You know, I think I'm beginning to get a complex," said Molly. She suddenly looked very serious.

"What's a 'complex'?" Tina asked.

"It's something that happens when someone picks on you. If they do it too much, you kind of go crazy. And that's called a complex. I think I might be getting one."

"I hope it's not catching," said Tina.

The front door opened and in walked Mr. and Mrs. Adams. Their arms were filled with paper bags and gaily-wrapped packages.

Mrs. Adams stamped the snow off her feet and said, "Hi, Tina. Did you girls have a nice afternoon? Molly, are you packed for tomorrow?"

"Yeah," Molly said. "I'm all ready to go. I'll pack my toothbrush in the morning. Thanks for the new pajamas."

"They're cute, aren't they?" asked Mrs. Adams. She shook her head. "I never thought I'd see you wearing pajamas with feet in them again, but Tina's mom says it gets pretty cold up in the hills."

"I guess I should go home and get my stuff together, too," said Tina. "We're going to have a great time!" she cried suddenly, hugging Molly. "You wait and see. You're probably a natural-born skier."

"I hope so," Molly said doubtfully. But she was excited, too. It made Ballard seem more like a real home, less strange. Going someplace with a friend made her feel like she belonged. Her heart beat quickly and Molly envisioned herself racing down ski slopes, sliding down hills and maybe even learning some fancy ski tricks.

Tina opened the front door. "Bye, everyone," she said. "We'll pick you up tomorrow morning around eight o'clock, okay?"

"Okay." Molly waved goodbye and Tina closed the door as she left.

41

"Well, you certainly have perked up," said Mrs. Adams. "Do you like Ballard more these days?" She smiled at Molly.

"Yeah. I guess so, now that I know Tina. This trip's going to be fun. That's for sure! We're going to sleep in bunk beds in the cabin and everything!"

"I'm glad to see all of you getting along so well," said Molly's dad, walking into the room. He shook the snowflakes out of his hair. "Your brother seems to like it here quite a bit. That basketball team has been a great help to him. Are you ready for the big game?"

"What big game?" Molly asked.

"It's still a few weeks away. But right after Christmas, Jeff is actually going to get to start in a game. The coach seems to think he's pretty good," her dad said.

"That's great," Molly said with a frown on her face. "Do I have to go?"

"Don't you want to see where your brother goes to school?" asked Mr. Adams. "I would think you'd like to see him play. It's a pretty big game, against Centerburg."

"I guess so," Molly said. She wondered, Whenever I hear an adult say, "I would think you'd like ..." the thing to like is always something I don't like. Why?

"Here's some mail," Mr. Adams said, handing

Molly an assortment of different colored envelopes. "Do you have a fan club back in Carlene?" He grinned and ruffled the top of her head with his hand.

"Oh, Dad. Give me a break," Molly said and grinned back. The sight of all those cards cheered her up. She took the envelopes to her room and opened them up one by one. Each was a Christmas card from a friend in Carlene: Vickie, Terry, Jim, Bonnie Sue, Della, Mary Louise, Donald, April, Rosemary, Carmen, and Brenda.

Molly set the cards around her, in a circle. She tried to pretend that the cards were the people who'd sent them and they were really there with her. But it didn't work. If anything, it was just the opposite and the circle of cards made the people seem farther away.

Molly tried to think about the ski trip. She knew that should cheer her up. But all she could think about was Carlene and how far away her friends were. It seemed strange to be happy one minute and then sad the next. But that was how it had been ever since she moved to Ballard. Was this all part of having a complex? she wondered. Was she going crazy? She sure hoped not. At least not before she went on the ski trip with Tina.

But more and more it seemed like she was

either laughing or crying, mostly crying. Sometimes Molly lay in bed at night and her eyes swelled with tears as soon as she thought about Ballard Junior High School and all of the gross, unfriendly kids who went there. Do I always have to cry or laugh? Isn't there anything in between? she wondered. Do all teenagers feel as I do?

But, Jeff was a teenager and he never looked like he was feeling down. Molly never saw him cry. And she bet that Jeff didn't lie in bed at night hoping for a tornado to come and knock his school down.

No. She, Molly Camilla Adams, was probably the only crazy one in the whole family. Maybe even in the whole town of Ballard!

Molly sighed. Her eyes filled with tears and she looked in her dresser mirror to see how sad she looked. The rims around her eyes turned pink. Her eyebrows were pushed down making a little wrinkle between her eyes. Her hair hung beside her cheeks framing the whole sad picture. In fact, she looked so sad that it made her sadder to see herself look that way. She squeezed her eyes shut and a tear trickled down over each cheek. She sniffed.

In the mirror's reflection Molly saw her math book on a chair behind her. She had to do four assignments in order to catch up with the rest of the class. But thinking about this didn't make

Molly sad. It made her mad.

"Why does everything happen to me?" she asked her reflection. "First, I have to move. Then I have to live in a pile of snow. And then I have to have Mr. Egghead for a teacher, which is giving me a complex. It's not fair!"

Molly turned and picked up the book. "I'm sick of looking at you," she said to the book's cover. Then she walked to her bed, lifted the mattress and slid the book as far back as she could. It made a rustling noise as it pressed against the math exams and unfinished homework hidden there.

Just then Molly heard Jeff come in the front door. "I'm home!" he called.

Mrs. Adams called from the kitchen, "Jeff, before you take your jacket off, would you get the grocery sack from the car, please?"

"Sure, Mom," Jeff answered.

Molly heard Jeff close the door as he walked back outside to the car.

Molly wondered how Jeff's afternoon had been. Did he get to sit by the red-haired girl at the Chili Parlor? Did he sit at a table laughing and joking with his friends?

Molly hoped that the red-haired girl thought Jeff's after-shave lotion smelled like sauerkraut.

Suddenly an idea popped into Molly's head. She knew what she wanted to do. She wanted to make a snowball and throw it, smack! onto Jeff's head. She wanted to get back at Jeff because he always got everything. Jeff had a million friends. Molly only had one. Jeff was on the basketball team. Molly had to give up cheerleading. Her parents were going to see Jeff play in a basketball game. But they weren't going to Molly's school because she wasn't on any team. *She* never did anything. Jeff liked Ballard. Molly hated it. Everything works out for Jeff, she thought. Nothing works out for me. Oh! It is just too much!

Molly jumped up and ran from her room to the front door. She threw it open and ran into the front yard. Jeff looked up in surprise. "What's going on?" he asked.

Molly picked up a handful of snow. It stung her bare hands as she packed it into a ball. She threw it hitting Jeff's shoulder. White powder spotted his jacket. But that wasn't good enough. She wanted to bounce one off his head.

Jeff began to laugh. "Now you're asking for it, Miss Smarty Pants," he said.

As he stooped to make a snowball, Molly threw another one. This one popped him right on the ear, knocking his cap into the snow. Molly shrieked with laughter. She turned and ran as Jeff chased her around the yard. He had a snowball in each hand. He threw one and it whizzed right over her head. Molly giggled wildly. Maybe this snow wasn't so bad after all, she thought. It was fun to play in . . .

Suddenly her right leg twisted and slid out at a crazy angle. Her other leg seemed to want to go in another direction. She fell and tumbled through the snow. A sharp pain shot through her ankle.

Jeff came running up, still laughing and said, "Hey, hot shot. I guess you'll think twice next time before you try to . . ." He stopped when he saw Molly's face. It was pale and her eyes were closed in pain.

"Mom! Dad!" he yelled. "Come quick!"

Mr. and Mrs. Adams came running from the house. "What's the matter here?" Mr. Adams asked breathlessly. "Oh, Molly!" He bent over Molly and picked her up in his arms. He carried her into the house where he laid her gently on the couch.

Molly sobbed quietly. Pain throbbed in her ankle and it seemed to get worse and worse. She wanted to scream.

"It looks like a bad sprain," said Mrs. Adams. "It's already beginning to swell." She touched Molly's ankle lightly with her finger.

"Ow-w!" yelled Molly. "Don't do that!"

"We'd better take her to the hospital," said Mr. Adams. "It might be broken. Jeff, you stay here with Wendy."

At the hospital the doctors in the Emergency Room looked at Molly's ankle. They X-rayed it.

Dr. Foley came into the examining room smiling. "Well, Miss Adams," she said. "You're a lucky girl. Nothing's broken. But you do have a sprain. Just keep that bandage on and stay off that foot for about two weeks. You should be able to walk on it around New Years."

"You mean I can't ski?" asked Molly.

Dr. Foley laughed. "Of course not. You'll have to be pretty still for the next week or so. We can get some crutches for you from the supply room."

* * * * * *

Mrs. Adams carried the crutches to the car. Mr. Adams carried Molly.

On the way home Molly tried to think of something besides the pain in her ankle. Mostly she thought about marshmallows and hot dogs roasting over a fire, sleeping in a bunk bed, riding on a sled and learning how to ski with Tina to help her. But thinking about those things didn't make her feel much better, so she looked out the window at the fast-moving, wintry landscape.

Why does everything happen to me? Molly wondered. I have the worst luck in the world.

And I have the worst big brother. This sprain is all his fault. If he hadn't made me so mad, I wouldn't have chased him in the snow. I wouldn't have fallen down and I'd still be going skiing with Tina tomorrow. It's Jeff's fault. *Everything* is Jeff's fault. He's ruining my life! And so is Mr. Egghead. He's ruining my life, too! *Everyone* is! The *whole world* is ruining my life!

My life was great before I moved to this ice cube town, Molly thought to herself. I really don't deserve all this bad luck. I'm nice to people. I try to be friendly and I'm kind of cute. So what's the problem? Why does my life stink?

Molly quietly broke into tears, her parents unaware.

6

Molly walked home from school as slowly as she could. She had two reasons for this. The first reason was that her ankle still hurt a little bit. It healed nicely over Christmas vacation, but she still had to be careful.

The second reason for walking so slowly was because she had her report card in her purse. She was embarrassed to show it to her parents. They would probably hit the roof when they saw that she had an *F* in math. An *F*!

She was pleased with her other grades, mostly *B*'s and an *A* in English. But even that *A* wouldn't make up for the *F*, not to her parents anyway. Molly had never failed a class in her life.

"Getting an *F* is worse than spraining my ankle," Molly muttered to herself. "In fact, if I could choose between getting an *F* and spraining my ankle, I'd choose the sprain. I'd rather walk barefoot in snow or live in an orange crate or set the table every night for two years or . . . *anything! Nothing* could be worse than getting an *F*." Molly shook her head and moaned out loud.

Molly knew she had to show the report card to her parents. She couldn't hide it under her mattress with all the other math tests she'd failed. Her bed was starting to make crinkly noises every time she sat on it.

She thought about erasing the *F* and writing in an *A*. But she knew her parents would find out. Mr. Egghead had told her that he was going to call them. He had to be the meanest man at Ballard Junior High School and probably the meanest teacher in the world!

Molly walked in zig-zags down the sidewalk. Walking took more time that way. Her toes were numb with cold. But frozen feet seemed better than listening to her parents yell at her.

When she got home, Molly laid her notebooks on the snow. She sat on the porch steps for five minutes before she went in. Jeff and Wendy were home as usual. Wendy was watching TV while Jeff pretended to dribble an imaginary ball around the living room. He leaped at the ceiling and shouted, "Two points!" Turning to Molly he said, "You ready for the big game tonight? You ready to see me win the game single-handedly?"

"What?" Molly asked in surprise. "What are

you talking about?"

"Don't tell me you forgot!" exclaimed Jeff. "You pea-brain! Tonight's my big night. We're playing basketball against Centerburg, and I'm in the starting line-up."

"Whoopee," said Molly without much enthusiasm. "How much did you pay the coach to let you play?"

Jeff threw a pillow at her, but Molly ducked just in time.

"We're home!" called Mrs. Adams. She and Mr. Adams walked in the front door, stamping the snow off their shoes.

Mrs. Adams kissed Wendy, then Molly, then Jeff. Her nose was red and cold.

"How was work, Mom?" asked Jeff.

"It's moving right along," she said, unbuttoning her furry coat. "I'm just about done with the bus program. Only a few more bugs to iron out and it'll be done."

Molly always thought it was funny to hear her mom call problems "bugs." And "ironing out a bug" sounded like a pretty squishy thing to do.

"How was work, Dad?" Molly asked.

"Oh, just another day at the salt mines," Mr. Adams said, grinning. He already had his feet in comfortable slippers. He sat beside Wendy in front of the TV and took a pipe from his pocket. He always smoked his pipe right before dinner. Molly liked the smell. The scent reminded her of cherries and vanilla mixed together.

"Aren't you excited, honey?" Molly's mother asked her. "We're going to see Jeff play tonight. I bet he's the best player on the team!"

And I'm the dumbest one in my math class, Molly thought to herself. She walked back to her room, closed the door and sat on her bed. A faint noise of tests and homework assignments came crackling from beneath the mattress.

Molly took the report card from her purse and looked at it again. The *F* was still there. That meant that this wasn't a nightmare. It was really happening.

But she *couldn't* show it to her parents right now, not now when they were so excited about Jeff's basketball game. Molly lifted the mattress and slid the bad news beneath it.

I'll tell them later, she thought. After the game. Or maybe tomorrow.

"Dinner!" she heard her mom call.

All through dinner Molly didn't say a word. She didn't feel like it. But she reasoned no one would notice because Jeff talked enough for everyone. He didn't eat because it was too close to the game. He talked about lay-ups, hook shots, slam-dunks, personal fouls and charging— basketball stuff. What else?

After dinner, the Adams family left for the high school. Mrs. Adams parked the car and they walked into the building. Molly noticed that

53

it looked a lot like her school, only bigger. Next year she would be out of junior high and coming here. She wondered what it would be like to be in the same school with Jeff.

As they walked down the hall, a tall boy wearing a jeans jacket came up. "Hey, Jeff, buddy," he said. "How's it going?" He clapped Jeff on the back.

It was like that all the way down the hall.

"Hi, Jeff!"

"Hey, Jeff. Good luck tonight!"

"Put in two for me, Jeff!"

"Hey, Adams! Chili Parlor after the game. Okay?"

A boy walked up saying, "Hi, Jeff. These your folks?"

"Yeah," said Jeff. "Mom and Dad, this is Gary Beggid. He's in my gym class."

"Hello, Gary," said Mr. Adams. "Good to meet you."

Molly stared at Gary. She wondered if he was Mr. Egghead's son. He didn't look like Mr. Egghead, though. His head wasn't bald and he wasn't holding a piece of chalk. Molly was glad when Gary walked on down the hall.

Then Jeff grabbed one guy by the arm and said, "Andy, I'd like you to meet my family. This is the first time they've been here. Here's my mom and dad. Dad, Mom, this is Andy White. He's the team captain."

"Hi," said Andy. He shook their hands.

"And these are my kid sisters," said Jeff.

"Hi," said Andy.

Molly couldn't believe it. Jeff didn't even tell Andy what her name was! And besides that, he said "kid sisters" as if she and Wendy were exactly alike. What an insult. She was 13 years old! That was eight years older than Wendy and they weren't anything alike. Wendy was still just a baby, and she, Molly Adams, was almost in high school! Is this how it's going to be next year when I come to this school? she wondered. Is everyone just going to think of me as Jeff's kid sister? He's the big basketball star and I'm a little nothing?

Molly followed her parents down the hall. She felt like a caboose on the end of a train.

"Here's the gym," said Jeff. "I've got to go!" He raced off down the hall with his gym bag in his hand.

The gymnasium was bright and warm. The floor shined under the lights. The bleachers were filling up and the school band was playing marching music from their section.

Molly's parents climbed up and sat near the center line on the Ballard Braves' side. They bought popcorn and soft drinks from a student-vendor and munched happily as they gazed around. Molly was kind of embarrassed to be seen with her parents. She wished that she was sitting with a group of girl friends. But since she didn't have a group of girl friends, that was impossible. Molly sighed. Then her eyes were drawn to the floor as a group of eight girls and eight boys ran out. It was the cheerleading squad wearing the red and white colors of the Braves.

Molly had never seen boy cheerleaders before. They didn't have them in Carlene. But it was neat. She watched them with interest. The boys held the girls up in the air and caught them when they turned flips. They all helped each other and they looked like they were having a great time.

Molly watched to see what kind of flips and jumps they did. I can do all that stuff, Molly thought happily. She daydreamed about next year. She would try out for cheerleading and she would make it. Then she'd teach them lots of new cheers, cheers she did in Carlene. Then she'd have a million friends just like Jeff. And no one would call her Jeff's kid sister.

Molly turned to see the clock on the wall. The game should be starting soon. Two people down, in the same row, sat a redheaded girl. She had the reddest hair and the greenest eyes Molly had ever seen.

That must be Jill, Molly thought. She's cute. I wonder what's wrong with her. Molly couldn't tell from looking. But something *had* to be wrong with her if she liked Jeff.

A buzzer buzzed so loudly that Molly jumped.

The Ballard Braves came running out from one end of the court and the Centerburg Tornadoes came from the other end. The crowd cheered and Molly couldn't help cheering along with them when she saw Jeff.

"Jeffie! Jeffie! Jeffie!" Wendy yelled, pointing down at the floor.

"There he is!" Mr. Adams shouted excitedly.

As the game began Jeff got the ball. He ran, dribbling the ball down the court. Another player jumped in front of him and Jeff was knocked to the floor. The basketball fell from his hands and rolled into the bleachers.

"Foul!" the Ballard fans called.

The referee called a foul on the other player. Jeff took two foul shots and made two baskets. The crowd cheered.

"Yea, Adams! Yea, Adams!"

"Go, Jeff!"

Molly heard the red-haired girl yell, "Go, Jeff! You can do it! Yea!"

Jeff played a great game. Molly was proud of him and envious at the same time. She was proud to be the sister of a basketball star. But Molly wished that people would cheer and yell for her, too. Well, next year they will, she thought. Next year I'll be a cheerleader! Well, she hoped she would be.

The Ballard Braves won the game by twelve points. Jeff made six baskets which was more than anyone else on the team.

Jeff showered, then met his family in the hall after the game.

"Mom, Dad," he said. "There's a victory celebration at the Chili Parlor. Want to come? Everyone's going to be there."

"Sure, let's go," said Mrs. Adams. "A bowl of hot chili sounds great."

"Why not?" said Mr. Adams. "How about you, Molly? Interested in some chili?"

"Sure," said Molly. She thought it might be fun to go somewhere with some older kids. They all seemed to be so friendly, to Jeff anyway.

"I want some chili," said Wendy.

"Okay, let's go." Mr. Adams drove to the Chili Parlor and they found a table. High school kids poured in and the place became crowded in no time.

Then the worst thing that could happen, happened. Mr. Beggid walked into the room. He was with Gary, the boy that Jeff had introduced earlier. Molly heard Gary say, "Dad, I'd like you to meet my new friend, Jeff Adams, and his family."

Molly had to think fast.

As Jeff and the Beggids came toward the Adams family, Molly dropped her napkin under the table. Then she scooted her chair out and leaned down as far as she could to get it. With her head under the table, she stared at her father's shoes and socks and wished she was some place where Mr. Beggid couldn't see her.

Molly stayed bent over, wondering how long she could pretend to be picking up a napkin. The blood rushed to her head and she felt warm.

Introductions were made and Mrs. Adams said, "Won't you join us?"

Mr. Beggid and Gary pulled chairs up to the table. Four more shoes with feet in them appeared under the table.

"Where's Molly?" asked Mrs. Adams.

Wendy giggled and lifted the tablecloth. "She's under here!" she said. "Molly's playing house. Can I go under here, too?"

"What in the world are you doing under there?" asked Mr. Adams with amazement in his voice.

"I dropped my napkin," Molly said quietly. She sat up and waved her napkin as proof.

Mr. Beggid stared at her, then looked at her parents, saying, "Oh, so you're *that* Adams. I'm afraid I've been meaning to call you about some rather unpleasant news. You have seen Molly's report card?"

Molly sat still, not moving a muscle, while the whole story came out. Mr. Beggid explained about her not doing her homework, about failing the tests. Finally he told about the *F* on her report card.

"Molly, why didn't you tell us? We could've

helped you," said her mother.

"Molly, I can hardly believe this," said her father.

"Did Molly do a boo-boo?" asked Wendy.

And Jeff just stared. He looked surprised. And, Molly thought, he looked disappointed. That really hurt. Molly was so proud of Jeff tonight when he led the basketball team to victory. But he'd never be proud of her, not now . . . not after he found out what a dummy she was.

No one was in a party mood anymore. They ate their chili quickly, then went home. Molly retrieved all her math papers and the report card from under her mattress. She showed them to her parents. For a minute she thought her mother was going to cry. She'd only seen her mother cry once, a long time ago, and that was at a movie.

"We'll have to think of a suitable punishment, Molly," said her mother. "We had no idea this was going on. You've been lying to us all this time."

Molly didn't say anything because she knew it was true.

Mr. Adams cleared his voice. Then he said, "Molly, unless you pull your math grade up to a C, you will not be allowed to visit Carlene next summer. And I mean that, young lady."

Tears rushed to Molly's eyes. Not go to Carlene? Not see Vickie, Terry, Jim, Bonnie

Sue, Della, Mary Louise, Donald, April, Rosemary, and . . . and . . .

"Oh, please!" Molly sobbed. "Let me go to Carlene. I hate it here! I really do!"

Mrs. Adams gently patted Molly's head. "We don't want to be mean," she said. "We're not doing this to hurt you. But you need to learn a lesson."

"Yes," said Molly's dad, in a kinder voice. "It's for your own good. Pull your grade up or . . . no Carlene next summer."

Molly ran to her room and slammed the door. She got her pajamas on and jumped into bed. It was quiet without the math papers rustling under the mattress. But still Molly didn't sleep very well.

Molly thought to herself, How come whenever parents say they don't want to hurt you, that's always when they're hurting you the most? It doesn't make sense.

At last Molly fell asleep. She dreamed she was being chased by a big 3. She jumped over a wall to escape, but a % tried to grab her and she could see a 57 coming from the other direction. She looked into the sky for help, but it was filled with 6's and 8's. And one of the 8's was bald and held a piece of chalk.

7

Molly ate breakfast quickly the next morning so she wouldn't have to look her parents in the eye. She felt terrible about lying to them. And she felt awful that they knew she flunked math. But she also felt a little better now that everything was out in the open, not *a lot* better, but a little.

She walked to school slowly, breathing in the cold air. In homeroom, she sat with a frown on her face and her eyes were red-rimmed from crying. The thought of not visiting Carlene in the summer was too "horful" to think about for very long. "Horful" was a word Molly made up when her head was under the table in the Chili Parlor. It was "horrible" and "awful" put together.

Molly tried to think of something happier, so she thought about cheerleading. She would try out in the spring. Then, if she made it, she would be a cheerleader at the high school. And she'd get to wear a beautiful red and white uniform. She knew she wasn't very good at math, but she was great at cheerleading. She'd show them all in the spring during tryouts.

The bell rang and as the rest of the class left the room, Mrs. Fister said, "Molly, can I see you a minute, dear?"

"Yes, ma'am," said Molly. She liked Mrs. Fister. Mrs. Fister was always nice to her and never yelled at her in front of the class like Mr. Beggid did.

"Molly, dear, is something bothering you?" asked Mrs. Fister. "You seem to be a million miles away this morning. What are you thinking about?"

"Cheerleading," said Molly. She didn't want to talk about all the other bad stuff because she knew she'd cry if she did.

"Cheerleading?" Mrs. Fister said. "Do you want to be a cheerleader?"

"Yes," said Molly. "I was a cheerleader in Carlene. I'm going to try out this spring."

"Well, dear, I think you'll make a lovely cheerleader," said Mrs. Fister smiling. "Just make sure to keep all your grades up. That's the only requirement that the high school has."

"What?" Molly's eyes stared, round with shock.

"The high school has a rule for its cheerleaders," Mrs. Fister said. "They can't have any

F's in any classes. If they do they're dropped from the squad."

"No *F*'s?" Molly couldn't believe what she was hearing.

"Not even one," said Mrs. Fister. "You'd better hurry, dear. You'll be late for your next class."

Molly walked slowly from the room. She was in a daze. She felt like a zombie. How can so many terrible things happen to one person? she wondered. I'm only 13 years old, but I feel like 100.

Her next class was English. She usually liked this class, but not today. Molly had too much on her mind. She didn't even notice when Arlene, who sat next to her, didn't say "hi."

Later that morning in math class, Molly stared dully at Mr. Beggid. She was too tired to be mad at him. And besides, there wasn't anything else he could do to her. He's already done every bad thing there was to do. Nothing was left, unless he made her shave her head and be bald like him.

"Before the bell rings today I would like to speak to you all about an important matter," said Mr. Beggid. "It concerns those of you who are having trouble keeping up with the rest of the class."

"Uh, oh," Molly whispered. She felt her ears flush pink. She didn't trust Mr. Beggid. What was he getting at?

"There is sometimes difficulty in the case of a transfer student," he continued. "That's simply because different schools cover different things. Some transfer students may move at a slower rate than others. But I believe we can deal with that problem."

Oh, no, thought Molly. Here it comes.

"I have decided to assign a tutor to those of you who need help," said Mr. Beggid. "The students who are making *A's* will work with the students who need help."

"Miss Adams," he said. "You will be working with Paul Derryvane. I've already spoken with Paul and he said he'd be glad to help you."

Molly turned to look at Paul sitting beside her.

Oh, no! Not him! she thought in horror. He's the brain who makes *A's* on every test. He's so pale and he has braces on his teeth! Oh, gross! *Anyone* but him! What a creep!

Paul turned to look at Molly and smiled.

He's laughing at me! She almost jumped up from her seat. Instead she looked straight ahead at the front of the classroom.

Molly felt all the other students staring at her. Probably, they would all talk about her later. And probably they all wanted to laugh at her right now.

Molly couldn't stand the idea of Paul tutoring

her. She thought to herself, They must think it's funny that I'm dumb and that Paul is such a creep. A dummy and a creep. What a great pair we make!

Mr. Beggid said, "Paul and Molly, I've made arrangements for you two to spend your study halls together in the library. That will be at three o'clock every day."

The bell rang. Molly wondered if there was a rule against throwing books at teachers. Probably there was.

The students squeezed through the door into the hall. Molly saw Paul in the crowd and she looked away from him. It was just too embarrassing. She didn't want anyone to see her with that creep. It was so hard to make new friends anyway. And if the other kids saw her hanging out with weird people, they'd think she was weird, too.

Molly and Tina walked down to the cafeteria. They got their trays, then sat at their usual place by the window. Not even the spaghetti that the cooks had made could cheer Molly up.

"Next thing you know he'll make me wear a sign on my back that says, 'BEWARE OF IDIOT!' " Molly complained.

"Oh, it's not so bad," said Tina. "You want to visit Carlene next summer, don't you? And what about cheerleading? You have to pull your grade up if you're going to do any of that. Maybe it's good that you have a tutor."

This was not what Molly wanted to hear. It was too practical. "Yuk!" was all she said.

Just then Arlene set her tray beside Tina's, then sat down.

"Hi," said Arlene. "What's happening?"

"Not much," said Tina.

"Hi," said Molly. She was always a little afraid to talk around Arlene. She just couldn't figure her out. It seemed that Arlene just didn't like her.

Molly tried to make conversation. "How'd you do on the English test?" she asked Arlene. "It was pretty easy, wasn't it? I wish math was as easy as English, don't you?"

Arlene stared with big blue eyes. They looked icy. "I did okay," she said. She turned back to Tina. "Do you want to go skating after school?" she asked. "My dad cleared the snow off the pond. It looks great. Jack and Tony are coming."

"Sure," said Tina. "How about you, Molly? Want to learn to ice skate?"

"I don't have any skates," said Molly.

"That's okay. You can try my mom's. Her feet are small," said Tina.

"Well, no thanks," Molly said. "I'd better not. I have to get home after school and watch Wendy. Maybe some other time." Molly really wanted to go. But she felt that Arlene should ask her since it was her pond. Arlene must not want her to come.

Molly ate her spaghetti in silence. She reminded herself about 3 o'clock and how she had to meet Paul in the library. She wasn't looking forward to that. In fact, she'd almost rather do *anything* else but that, even eat sauerkraut. Yuk!

But 3:00 came and Molly slowly made her way to the library. She saw Paul sitting at a table back in a corner. He's probably hiding, she thought. He doesn't want to be seen with me any more than I want to be seen with him. She walked over to the table.

"Hi!" said Paul. He jumped up and pulled out a chair for Molly. Molly noticed that he was pretty tall. He might even be taller than Jeff and Jeff was a basketball player.

"Hello," said Molly sullenly. She sat down putting her notebook and math book on the table.

Paul sat across from her and stared, smiling. His braces shined bright and silvery.

Molly looked around to see if anyone was watching. Hopefully, she thought, no one will see us together. It might ruin my reputation. It then occurred to Molly that she didn't have a reputation to ruin. But, she reasoned, *if* I had one, it would be terrible to be seen with this tin-grin boy, and that is close enough. Then I'll *never* be popular.

Paul was still smiling. "How can I help you out?" he asked. "I know it must be rough, coming to a new school in the middle of the year. There's bound to be some catching up to do."

"It's not so bad," Molly said. She didn't want to admit how sad and lonely she got sometimes. Anyway, she didn't want this guy to feel sorry for her.

The library door opened and Molly looked up. In walked Arlene and Tony Ramado. Tony was a member of the Ballard Junior High Ski Team. Everyone said he was going to be a professional some day. He was so cute. He looked like one of those good-looking guys in a sunglasses commercial, and, even though it was the middle of winter, he had a golden tan.

Tony and Arlene walked by Paul and Molly's table. Arlene didn't say anything, but Tony said, "Hi, Paul."

"Hi, Tony," Paul said and smiled his silvery smile.

Arlene and Tony sat down at another table. Arlene whispered something in Tony's ear and he began laughing.

I'll bet they're laughing at us, Molly thought. They probably think I like this goofy guy. Gross!

"Where should we start?" Paul asked. He

opened the math book. "What are you having the most trouble with?"

Molly explained that she was having trouble with everything. She and Paul went back to the very first homework assignment and began studying. After an hour it was time to quit. Molly closed the book and began to leave. But first Paul said, "I hear you're from Arizona. I traveled through there once with my parents. It's a beautiful state."

"Oh, it is!" Molly exclaimed. "I love the desert. I love the sunshine!" Then she remembered who she was talking to and said, "Bye."

"Just a second," said Paul. "Want to go out for a pizza this Saturday? My older brother can drive us."

"No thanks," said Molly. She wouldn't be caught dead with this guy.

"Are you sure?" asked Paul. "Some of the other kids are going, too—Tony, Arlene, Josh, and Fran."

"Uh, well, okay." Molly changed her mind. She figured that this would be the perfect chance to meet some new kids. She hated for her first date in Ballard to be with such a nerd, but maybe she'd meet someone better.

"Great!" said Paul. "I'll pick you up at eight o'clock. See ya." He smiled.

Molly stared at his braces. "See ya," she said.

At dinner that night Mrs. Adams squeezed Molly's hand under the table. She said, "I'm glad you're going out, honey. I think you'll be happier once you know a few more people."

"How's tutoring going?" Mr. Adams asked. It seemed to Molly that her dad was trying to be extra nice to her ever since the whole report card mess. Probably he felt bad for yelling at her.

"It's going okay, Dad," she said.

"Who are you going out with?" asked Jeff. "Maybe I should come along to make sure you don't do anything dumb," he snorted with laughter.

"Oh, be quiet!" said Molly. "Don't call me dumb. His name's Paul Derryvane."

"Is he your boyfriend?" asked Wendy.

Molly shook her head. "This family is really weird," she said. "Brothers and sisters can be such a pain."

Molly was nervous about Saturday and going out with Paul. But she tried not to show it. She hoped that he'd take his braces off and lie under a sunlamp.

The next day in homeroom, Molly whispered to Tina. "Do you know Paul Derryvane?"

"Yes," Tina whispered back. "He's in our class."

"Is he the biggest nerd in the school?"

"No!" Tina said in a surprised voice. "Why do

71

you ask that?"

"Because he seems kind of nerdy to me," said Molly. "But I'm going out with him this Saturday. I can't believe I said 'yes.' I think I must be crazy or something."

"You're crazy to think he's a nerd. I think he's real nice," said Tina. "He's real smart, too."

I don't know. I just don't know, Molly muttered to herself as she hurried to science class. He looks kind of goofy to me. But maybe I'll meet some other kids, at last!

8

When Saturday came, Molly spent the whole afternoon trying on everything in her closet. It wasn't so much for Paul. After a week of being tutored, Molly still thought he was a terrible jerk. But she wanted to look good for Arlene, Tony, and the other kids. There's no telling how many new people she might meet, especially cute guys!

At last, Molly decided on a cream and red plaid skirt with a matching cherry-red sweater. It looked nice with her blonde hair.

She wore a silver Indian bracelet from New Mexico and braided her hair with cream satin ribbons. A touch of red lip gloss completed the picture.

"Wow!" Jeff exclaimed when Molly came out from her room. "You smell like you fell in some bug spray."

Molly had dabbed just a little lavender cologne behind her ears. She began to punch Jeff on the arm, but stopped because she didn't want to get messed up.

Molly's dad stood up and put his glasses on when she came into the living room. "Oh, my!" he exclaimed. "My little girl grew up when I wasn't looking! Molly, you're quite the young lady," he said, bowing.

"Oh, Dad," said Molly. But secretly she was pleased.

"Good heavens!" said Mrs. Adams. "You look great!"

"You're beautiful, like a movie star!" shrieked little Wendy.

"Gee! What's the big deal about?" exclaimed Molly. "Do I usually look like a frog or something?"

"Of course not, dear," said Mrs. Adams.

"Yes," said Jeff. "A bullfrog." He smiled. "No, really, Sis," he said. "You look foxy. You'll knock old Paul's eyes out when he sees you."

"Thanks," said Molly. She was glad to have Jeff's approval. But, suddenly she felt shy.

Then the doorbell rang. For an instant, everyone stood still. Mr. Adams walked to the foyer and opened the door. There stood Paul. He didn't look half-bad. His blue eyes sparkled. But then he ruined his looks by smiling and showing his braces.

"Come in, Paul. Glad to meet you." Mr.

Adams opened the door wider and stood back to let Paul pass. A gust of cold wind came in with him.

Mrs. Adams offered Paul a chair in the living room. He sat down after first saying hello to Molly.

"Hi," said Jeff. "I'm Molly's brother. Haven't I seen you somewhere before?"

"Sure," Paul said. "I remember you down at the high school gym. I practice there sometimes with the older guys."

"Hey!" exclaimed Jeff. "That's it! You're a basketball player, aren't you? You're pretty good, too! I've seen you. Do you play at the junior high school?"

"Yeah," said Paul. "I'm captain of the team this year."

"Well, this is a surprise. Molly never told us you played basketball," said Mrs. Adams.

"That's because I didn't know," said Molly. She was just as surprised as her mother.

"I've been working on my slam-dunks," Jeff said to Paul. They both laughed at that. "Maybe we can get together and play on Saturday," Jeff suggested.

"Sure," said Paul. "I'd like that."

"I hear you work at the Smith-Glass plant," Paul said to Mr. Adams. "How do you like it there?"

"Oh, I can't complain. I know the personnel there well. And sales are up. All in all, it's a very satisfying job."

"And you're into computers?" Paul asked, turning to Mrs. Adams. "Molly tells me you're a programmer. What exactly do you do?"

"I just wrote a program for the bus company," said Mrs. Adams. "It figures out gasoline usage and mileage for each bus. Now I'm starting one that will help out the payroll people at BTC."

"Are you using a micro computer?" Paul asked.

"No. There wouldn't be enough file space or memory. We're using a mini," said Mrs. Adams.

"What kind?"

"A Vax-730."

"What's it written in?"

"BASIC and Assembler. My! You certainly seem to know a lot about computers. Are you a computer buff?"

"I hack around some," said Paul. "I have a computer at home."

Molly thought, There goes mom talking about computers again. Chinese and numbers, that's what it sounds like to me. I can't believe Paul understands that stuff!

Paul turned to Molly and said, "My computer's a micro-mini-mainframe."

So what? Molly thought. It could be a micro-

Minnie-Mouse for all I know.

"We'd better be going," said Paul. "My brother's waiting in the car. We'll be at the Village Pizza Inn," he told Mr. and Mrs. Adams.

Molly pulled on a warm coat and left with Paul. Jeff called after them, "Don't forget, Paul. Basketball next Saturday at 12 noon in the gym. Okay?"

"Okay!" Paul called back.

Paul's brother John seemed nice. He told Paul that he was going to drop them off at the pizza place. Then he was meeting some friends at a movie. Afterward, he'd come and pick them up again.

Molly and Paul climbed out of the car and crossed a slushy sidewalk in front of the Village Pizza Inn. Pink lights glowed around the front window.

Arlene and Tony were already sitting at a round table. Josh and Fran were there, too. A candle flickered from the table's center, casting shadows on their faces. "Hi, Paul," they all said.

Molly wondered why they all seemed to like Paul so much. They didn't even seem to notice his braces. In Carlene there was a guy with braces in her class and everyone called him "tin grin," "brace face" or "railroad tracks." But nobody in Ballard called Paul names. And they didn't even notice how pale he was. She noticed that nearly no one had tans like her friends back in Carlene.

Molly was excited to be with these people. Maybe Arlene, the snob, would talk to her for a change.

"Everyone, this is Molly Adams," said Paul. "She moved here from Carlene, Arizona. Molly, this is Tony, Arlene, Josh, and Fran. They're all crazy, so be careful." He winked at the group and they all laughed.

Molly and Paul sat down with the others at the table with the red-checkered tablecloth. They ordered a large pizza with everything on it except anchovies.

The others seemed to talk and chatter easily about school, classes, sports, records, skiing and skating. But, suddenly Molly felt shy. She wished that Tina was there with her. Molly was on her own now. She had to make friends with these people. She knew she couldn't cling to Tina forever. What if Tina moved? Molly knew she had to make new friends. But she just couldn't think of anything to say.

As if sensing her discomfort, Paul tried to help her out by bringing her into the conversation.

"Molly used to be a cheerleader," he said to Arlene. "You girls have that in common, don't you? I'll bet you both have lots of cheerleading stories to tell, right?"

"Sure," said Molly. "I told Arlene before that I was a cheerleader for two years in Carlene. I just loved it. I hope I can try out next year. Don't you love being a cheerleader, Arlene?" Molly asked.

"Girl talk," said Josh making a face. "We'll let you two talk about cheerleading while we play the video games. Anyone interested?"

"Sure," said Fran. "Since I'm not a cheerleader, I'd rather play the video games than talk about pom-poms and stuff." She smiled.

"I'll play," said Tony, standing up.

"Yeah, me too," said Paul. "I can tell these two have a lot to talk about."

The rest of the group went into the video room next door, leaving Molly and Arlene alone.

Molly was glad to get a chance to talk to Arlene about cheerleading. Maybe now they could get to know each other.

"We had six kinds of jumps we used," she said. "And we did pom-pom routines, too. I think those were my favorite."

Arlene just stared at her, not saying a word. Molly began to feel a little uneasy. But she kept talking.

"Our uniforms were yellow and blue," she said. "Yellow for the sun and blue for the sky. You know, if I make cheerleading next year I'll..."

"If you want to be a cheerleader so much, why don't you just move back to your precious

Carlene?" cried Arlene suddenly.

Molly's mouth hung open for a second. She couldn't believe it.

Arlene's face turned red as she continued. "I'm so tired of hearing about you and your stupid Carlene, I could scream!" she said. "That's all you ever talk about. Carlene and cheerleading, Carlene and cheerleading, and how much you miss them. All you ever think about is yourself! What a selfish snob you are!"

Molly was stunned. Her eyes filled with tears. Then she jumped up and ran into the ladies restroom. She stood by the towel dispenser sobbing. Molly's shoulders heaved with each violent breath.

This is the last straw! Molly thought. I was just trying to be friendly. And what does Arlene do? Arlene says all kinds of nasty things to me. Why? Is there something terribly wrong with me that I don't know about? Why does everyone hate me? What is it?

The bathroom door opened and in walked Arlene. Her hands were trembling and her cheeks were flushed.

Molly stared at Arlene through tearful eyes. Suddenly she blurted out, "Why do you hate me? What have I ever done to you?"

"Hate you?" Arlene exclaimed. Her eyes widened with surprise. "I could ask *you* the same question." Arlene asked, "Why do YOU hate ME?"

"Wh-wh-what?" Molly stuttered. She was shocked. "What makes you think I hate *you*?" she asked.

Arlene hung her blonde head, looking sadly down at the floor. "Because you're always asking me about cheerleading and English," she said. "Everyone knows I'm flunking English. And if I don't pull my grade up, I won't get to try out for the high school squad next year."

Molly looked closely at Arlene. She'd been so busy crying that she hadn't noticed how upset Arlene was. "I didn't know," Molly said earnestly. "Honest, I didn't."

"I thought everyone knew," said Arlene. "I thought you were glad I was flunking because that would give you a better chance of becoming a cheerleader. I know you want to try out. You've talked so much about being a cheerleader in Carlene."

"No!" said Molly. "I didn't mean to hurt your feelings. I didn't want to throw you out of the cheerleading squad. I was just trying to think of things to talk about."

"I've thought you were a terrible snob ever since you moved here," said Arlene.

Molly couldn't believe her ears. Was Arlene really saying all this stuff? Her? Molly Adams? A snob? No way! She'd never had a snobby day in her life! Not her! Not Molly Adams!

"Why did you think I was a snob?" asked Molly. She stared into Arlene's blue eyes, waiting for an answer.

"You never come to any of the games at school," said Arlene. "You don't seem to want to do things with the other kids."

"I'm just shy, that's all," said Molly. But she wondered to herself, Am I really a snob? Maybe that's why Jeff has so many friends and I don't. He joined the basketball team. He goes to the Chili Parlor and meets new people. He gets out there and tries things: skiing, skating, sledding. Molly suddenly realized, with a shock, that she'd never been to one single basketball game at her own school. That's why she didn't know Paul was a basketball player. She hadn't gone to any of the other sports events or Pep Rallies either.

I've never even seen the cheerleaders cheer, she thought to herself. Maybe I haven't tried hard enough to be friendly. I didn't even want to go out with Paul tonight because he has braces. And when I think about it I really do like him. He's awfully nice. And there's nothing wrong with having braces. Maybe Arlene's right! Maybe *I'm* the snob! Me! Molly Camilla Adams, the snob!

All these ideas whirled in Molly's head. It felt

like a whole merry-go-round of troubles and questions twirling between her ears. But, how could she stop it?

"I can help you," Molly suddenly blurted out. "I know I can."

"What?" asked Arlene.

"English is my very best subject," said Molly. "I'll tutor you. We can meet after school at my house. Okay?"

"You're just offering that because you feel sorry for me. You think I'm dumb," said Arlene sadly.

Once again, Molly was surprised. Arlene was thinking the very same thoughts Molly used to think, about people thinking she was dumb because she had a tutor. Molly thought about how funny and odd it was to find out that pretty cheerleaders with blonde hair and blue eyes have the same problems that everyone else has. They flunked classes, too, and wondered if other kids thought they were dumb.

"I don't think you're dumb at all!" Molly exploded. "I think *I'm* dumb for ever thinking you thought I was dumb when really . . . Oh, I don't know!" Suddenly she began to giggle. Arlene giggled, too.

"You know, it's really pretty funny when you think about it," said Molly. She leaned back against the sink. "Here we are, both flunking a subject and afraid that everyone's laughing at us. We're both afraid of winning the Miss Dumb America award. I guess if anything is dumb, it's me thinking that I'm dumb when I know I'm not. I'm just having some trouble with a class, that's all."

"Yeah," said Arlene. "It really is pretty silly. Everybody needs help now and then. I'll take you up on that tutoring offer. If you tutor me in English, I'll help you with cheerleading. I can teach you some of the cheers they do at the high school. You might need to know them for tryouts."

"That would be great!" said Molly. "But I've got to pass math first or else . . ." She pulled a finger across her throat and made a squawking noise.

Arlene stretched her hand out in front of herself. "Put it there, pardner," she said.

Molly took Arlene's hand and shook it as a sign that a new friendship was just beginning.

Right then a gray-haired woman opened the bathroom door and walked in. She looked at the two red-eyed girls who stood with their arms stretched out and hands clasped.

"Excuse me," said the woman.

They giggled as they dropped their hands and let the woman pass. She went into a stall and closed the door.

Molly and Arlene turned on the cold water

and began to splash their faces, trying to get the red out.

"She must think we look pretty weird," whispered Molly.

Arlene giggled. "The others will think we're weird, too, when they see how our eyes are all puffed up. They'll think we punched each other out or something." Arlene took a compact out of her purse and dabbed the powder puff around her eyes. Then she handed it to Molly. "Here," she said. "How do I look?"

"Great!" answered Molly. "How do *I* look?"

"Like you walked into a door," said Arlene. "No, I'm just kidding," she said when she saw Molly's worried expression.

Molly and Arlene hurried out the door and back to their table. The others were sitting around a large pizza and Paul was cutting it up into slices.

"Hey," he said. "Where've you been?"

"Why do girls always go to the bathroom together?" asked Josh.

"I was afraid you fell in and got flushed away," said Tony.

"Oh, Tony!" said Arlene. "You're gross."

"See? I knew you two would have a lot to talk about. Right?" said Paul.

Arlene and Molly looked at each other and smiled. The candlelit room was dark enough to hide their red eyes and flushed cheeks.

But they knew. They knew that they'd just shared a private, close time together. And that's how friendships begin. They knew that the talk they'd had in the bathroom was nothing like the talk Paul thought they'd had. Little did he know about the tears and tempers that had just exploded. It was really kind of funny when you thought about it.

First Arlene giggled. Then Molly started in. It seemed like they couldn't stop. Molly realized that five minutes ago she was crying just as hard as she was laughing now.

"You girls are weird," said Josh, passing pizza pieces around. "I'm glad guys aren't weird like girls."

"Anyone got a quarter?" asked Fran. "Let's play some tunes on the jukebox." As she was selecting songs and punching buttons, Paul leaned toward Molly. He whispered in her ear, "I think you're pretty."

Molly looked around to make sure no one had heard. She was kind of embarrassed and tried very hard to think of something to say back to Paul.

She couldn't tell him he was cute, because she didn't think he was. At last Molly leaned over and whispered in his ear, "I think you're very tall."

9

Molly sat at her writing table with a sheet of white paper before her. She wrote:

Dear Vickie,

You should see spring here. It's really different from Carlene. It's green everywhere. The snow's finally melted and I can see our yard for the first time. We have tiny violets in the front yard and red, yellow and white tulips in the backyard. There are birds chirping all over the place, too. They wake me up every morning, like an alarm clock. But I don't mind. I kind of like them.

Last weekend I went to the movies with Tina, Arlene, and Fran. It was a stupid movie about a girl who lived in a cave with some chickens. It was called Mountain Cave Girl. If you ever get a chance to see it. DON'T! Talk about weird!!!

Paul's coming over today. We're going to ride our bikes down to Leevy's pond. It's still too cold to swim. but Paul's got an extra fishing rod. I hope I don't have to put worms on the hook .

Jeff's been helping me with my math. So has Paul. I think he's a genius (Paul. NOT Jeff) but I would never tell him that. I got B's on the last three tests I took. I've been working really hard. Math is still kind of like torture to me. but I think that's because I have a complex and it's really not so bad. I swear. if I ever get an A in math. I'll have a heart attack. My average is a C now, so I'll be able to try out for cheerleading. Tryouts are this Wednesday after school! Me, nervous? You bet! But I'm excited and not even Mr. Egghead can stop me now!

I have an idea. Tell me what you think of it. Instead of me staying for two weeks in Carlene this summer, how about if I stay one week and then you come up to Ballard for a week? I think you'd like it here. It's really pretty. You won't believe the rolling green hills and all the trees. Plus, I'd like you to meet my friends, especially Tina. She's almost as crazy as you are!!!

Let me know if you can come. Please say "hi" to Brenda Vosta for me.

Your Minnesotan friend,
Molly

Molly folded the letter and put it in an envelope. She also put in a photo of herself and Paul at the school's spring picnic. Tina had taken the picture while she and Paul sat out on the school lawn eating lunch together.

In the photo, Molly has her mouth full of potato salad. But it was a good picture of Paul. His braces didn't bother her so much anymore. Molly was trying very hard not to be a snob. It wasn't easy sometimes, especially when she saw a kid with pointy ears, bushy eyebrows, glasses and too-short-red-pants with green tennis shoes. But Molly just thought back to her first day at Ballard Junior High School when she wore the wrong kind of shoes and slipped in the slush. When she remembered sitting in that puddle in homeroom with all the class laughing at her, she didn't feel like putting anyone down.

Molly counted the days until cheerleading tryouts. They were to be held in the Ballard High School gym. She practiced her cheers every day at home with her family as an audience. Of course, Jeff had to say something mean, like she should join the circus. But then he'd smile and say, "Just kidding. You're doing great, Sis. I really mean it."

Her parents clapped and told her when she looked good and what she could improve. Wendy held a glass of ice water for her while she practiced. Sometimes Arlene came over and they practiced together.

"Now, Molly," her mother said to her one night. "I know how much your heart is set on becoming a cheerleader, but not everyone who tries out can make it, so . . ."

"I know, Mom," said Molly. "Don't worry. Whatever happens, I can take it." But Molly wondered. What if I don't make it? I hope I don't cry! No! I'd never do that! It would be too embarrassing!

At last the day for tryouts came and Molly went to the high school. It seemed so big as it always did. It was hard to believe that she'd be going to school there next year.

Arlene was waiting in the gym when Molly got there. Fran and Tina came to watch. They both promised to clap loudly when Molly and Arlene went out on the floor to show their cheers. They looked at the older girls around them. Some of next year's sophomores, juniors and seniors were trying out for the squad, too. Molly thought they looked so smart and cool, like girls in magazines.

When Arlene's name was called, she ran out on the floor before the judges table. She performed her cheer and showed her three best jumps. Then she ran off the floor. She looked great. Molly thought she would become a high school cheerleader for sure!

Fran and Tina clapped and cheered. One of the judges turned and said, "If you two girls can't be quiet, we'll have to ask you to leave." Tina and Fran were embarrassed. So they sat very quietly after that.

"Molly Adams!"

Even though she was expecting her name to be called, Molly jumped a little in her seat when she heard it. "Molly Adams!" the judge called again.

Molly ran out onto the floor. Her hair brushed against her shoulders with each step.

Molly put her hands on her hips and stood with her legs together and knees slightly bent.

"For my cheer," she said, "I'm going to do one I learned in Carlene, Arizona."

Molly jumped and shouted. She arched her back and bent her arms at the elbows. She did the liveliest cheer she knew and kept a smile on her face the whole time. She pretended that she was cheering for Jeff and Paul during next year's basketball season. When she was done she did a straight jump, a deer jump and an eagle jump. When Molly landed after the eagle jump, her ankle wobbled a bit and she had to take an extra step. It was the same ankle she had sprained right before Christmas.

It's just my luck for it to act up now when I

really need it to be strong! she thought.

Molly ran off the floor and sat once again with Tina, Arlene, and Fran. "I blew it!" she moaned. "I just know I did!"

"Maybe they won't count that one mistake," said Arlene. But she looked worried.

There were about thirty girls trying out for eight cheerleading spots. The boys' tryouts were planned for Friday.

The girls waited as the judges added their scores.

"I can't believe we'll be freshmen next year," said Tina. "It seems so old, doesn't it?"

"Yeah," said Fran. "But we'll be the youngest in the school . . . the babies. Ugh!"

"It's going to be scary," said Tina. "I hope the upperclassmen aren't mean or anything."

"I think they all have sharp teeth, green hair and claws," joked Fran.

"Probably they'll make us do their homework for them," said Arlene.

"Then they'll flunk for sure!" Molly giggled.

"Attention, ladies!" The voice of the head judge cut through the chatter in the bleachers.

"We have selected our new squad for next year," she said. The judge hesitated, then went on. "The Ballard Braves' cheerleaders for next year are Nicole Paine, Sue Ann Johnson, Paulette Snopes, Arlene Schwartz, Ann Murphy, Sue

Price, and Bethany Dodridge. You all did a fine job. Congratulations, girls. We'll be contacting you to let you know about uniforms and practice."

A girl sitting behind Molly began to cry. Molly felt like crying, too, but she wanted Arlene to know that she was happy for her. She didn't want to ruin Arlene's big day.

"Congratulations," said Molly, hugging Arlene. "I really mean that. Honest, I do."

Arlene, Tina, and Fran felt bad for Molly. They all knew how much being a cheerleader meant to her. They put their arms around her. They said, "Please don't feel bad, Molly. You can try again next year."

Molly felt the good wishes and friendship that they felt for her. She knew that even though she didn't make cheerleading, she was a very lucky girl. She turned to leave the gym.

"Hey! Wait a minute!" Tina yelled suddenly, pulling away. She called down to the judge, "That's only seven! There should be eight cheerleaders, right?"

"My heavens!" exclaimed the head judge. She shuffled through the papers in her hand. "You're right. Oh, here it is. Girls! Girls! There's been a mistake. I'm terribly sorry. Our eighth cheerleader is Miss . . . Miss . . . Oh, here it is. Miss Molly Adams! We almost forgot you. Sorry, Molly."

"Yea!" cheered Tina, Fran and Arlene, jumping up and down. They surrounded Molly and began hugging her.

"Wow!" said Molly. "Am I dreaming? Is this for real?"

"Let's check," said Tina. "How about if we all pinch you?"

"No," Molly laughed. "I guess it's real. I'm a cheerleader! Wait until I tell my parents! Wait until I tell Paul!"

The girls looked around and noticed that everyone else had left. While they stood there yelling and congratulating each other, the gymnasium had emptied. The winners had rushed off to celebrate and tell their friends the good news. The losers had hurried off to their homes to hide their disappointment. The four girls were the only people left in the gym. It stretched around them now, huge and silent.

"It's spooky in here," said Tina. "It's so big."

"It's going to be really weird next year," Fran said shivering. "We won't know anyone."

"I know what you mean," said Arlene. "I'm kind of scared, too. It could be pretty awful coming to a new school and feeling so lost and alone. All the upperclassmen will already have friends. We'll be the *new* girls. Yuk!"

Suddenly, the three girls looked at Molly. Molly just stood and smiled a happy smile. "It's not so bad," she said. "We'll all have each other. And besides, being a new girl can be fun. I ought to know."

Molly winked at them. The four friends left the gymnasium, their footsteps echoing around them. Each girl had a daydream in her head, a hope for the coming school year and what it would bring.

Molly's dream was filled with pictures of red and white uniforms, Pep Rallies, her parents watching her from the bleachers, *B*'s in math, ice-skating, learning to ski and of course, Paul. There was no bald-headed person holding a piece of chalk in Molly's dream. And of course, there was no sauerkraut.

Yes, there was a new school to go to, and a new year ahead of her. Molly Adams could hardly wait!